THE CHRISTMAS FEAST:

A Fishy Tale

Diana Pishner Walker

Headline Kids
an imprint of Headline Books, Inc.
Terra Alta, WV

The Christmas Feast—A Fishy Tale

by Diana Pishner Walker

illustrations by Headline Kids Group

copyright ©2021 Diana Pishner Walker

To order additional copies of this book or for book publishing information, or to contact the author:

Headline Kids
P. O. Box 52
Terra Alta, WV 26764

Tel: 304-789-3001
Email: mybook@headlinebooks.com
www.headlinebooks.com

Published by Headline Books
Headline Kids is an imprint of Headline Books

ISBN-13: 9781951556372

Library of Congress Control Number: 2020943836

PRINTED IN THE UNITED STATES OF AMERICA

This book is dedicated to Father Chris Turner
and in memory of Father Benedict Kapa.

I would also like to dedicate this book in memory of a
very special Uncle, Joseph Allessio. This will be the first
Christmas Eve that we will not be able to share our talk,
hugs and special Italian foods.

My family continues to celebrate each Christmas Eve,
with the Feast of the 7 Fishes.

At the time of this printing our world as we know it is in
crisis. I hope this story brings to light the true meaning
of hope, family and a community coming together to
help each other in a great time of need.

BUON NATALE !

Benny and Turner were cousins who lived in a small fishing village in Italy.

Their papas were brothers, and for generations the families had lived side by side in the same two houses.

Each day, Benny, whose real name was Bernardo, and Turner, who was nicknamed because he got to turn the wheel in the fishing boat, went to school and then to the sea to fish. While their papas were out at sea, they patiently waited on the shore with their fishing poles to be picked up.

Big smiles appeared on their faces when they saw the family boat coming close to shore. They boarded the boat with their papas and threw their lines into the sea. Fishing was a family business. It not only provided many tasty meals, but it was also a busy business in the market square.

Every Sunday after church
both families took the fish to the
market to be sold. There was more than
enough to feed the whole village!

During the Christmas season there was even
more fish to be caught and sold in the market for the
Feast of the Seven Fishes on Christmas Eve.

The Feast of the Seven Fishes

Squid

Calamari

Clams

Shrimp

Lobster

Baccala

The Feast had always been a Christmas tradition for many families in the Italian village. On Christmas Eve they celebrated with a huge meal which included 7 different kinds of fish!!But one Christmas season Turner's papa became ill. He was not able to help catch the fish and Benny's papa hurt his leg. So he wasn't able to fish either.

Benny and Turner decided it was up to them to take the boat out to sea alone, without permission, and catch the fish for the Feast.

While on the boat, they cast their fishing lines and threw out nets, just like their papas. But then the storm came.

The boat began to rock.

The rain and snow fell so hard they could not see each other. They could not fish. They were cold and wet, scared, and hungry. How would they get home on this Christmas Eve? They knew that by now their mamas, papas and all of the people of the village would be worried. They were in so much trouble!

Benny and Turner held each other tight as they began to shiver, then cry.

All of a sudden, they saw a very bright light in the sky. They thought it was coming from the lighthouse where the old lady Lucia lived but even the light house was dark.

It seemed to calm the storm. Benny looked up and pointed to the sky. "My dear cousin it's a star, it's guiding us."

It warmed their cold, shivering little bodies. They forgot how hungry they were. They were now able to see the shore and all of the villagers waiting, some with blankets, to welcome them from the storm.

Turner's dad was there on crutches and Benny's dad was there in a chair wrapped with many blankets. Benny thought "Oh no! Papa is too ill to be out in the storm!"

As they pulled up alongside the shore, everyone began to cheer! Their mamas wrapped them in blankets. They heard one of the villagers say "Now we will feast on this blessed Christmas Eve."

"How?" Turner thought out loud. "We have NO fish! We could not save Christmas Eve! It is ruined!"

Benny answered as he looked around the floor of the fishing boat, "Ummmm….Turner…"

"The boat is full of fish!"

The villagers enjoyed the feast all together in the town hall. They could not have asked for more.

Benny's papa announced, "Benny and Turner… we are so happy you are safe. But you must understand on this stormy night that Christmas Eve will come with or without the feast. If you are ever in trouble again, and you had better not be, the Christmas Star will guide you every night, not just on Christmas Eve."

Music played and the feast began!

At midnight, everyone went to church together.

Benny and Turner never took the boat out without their papas again.

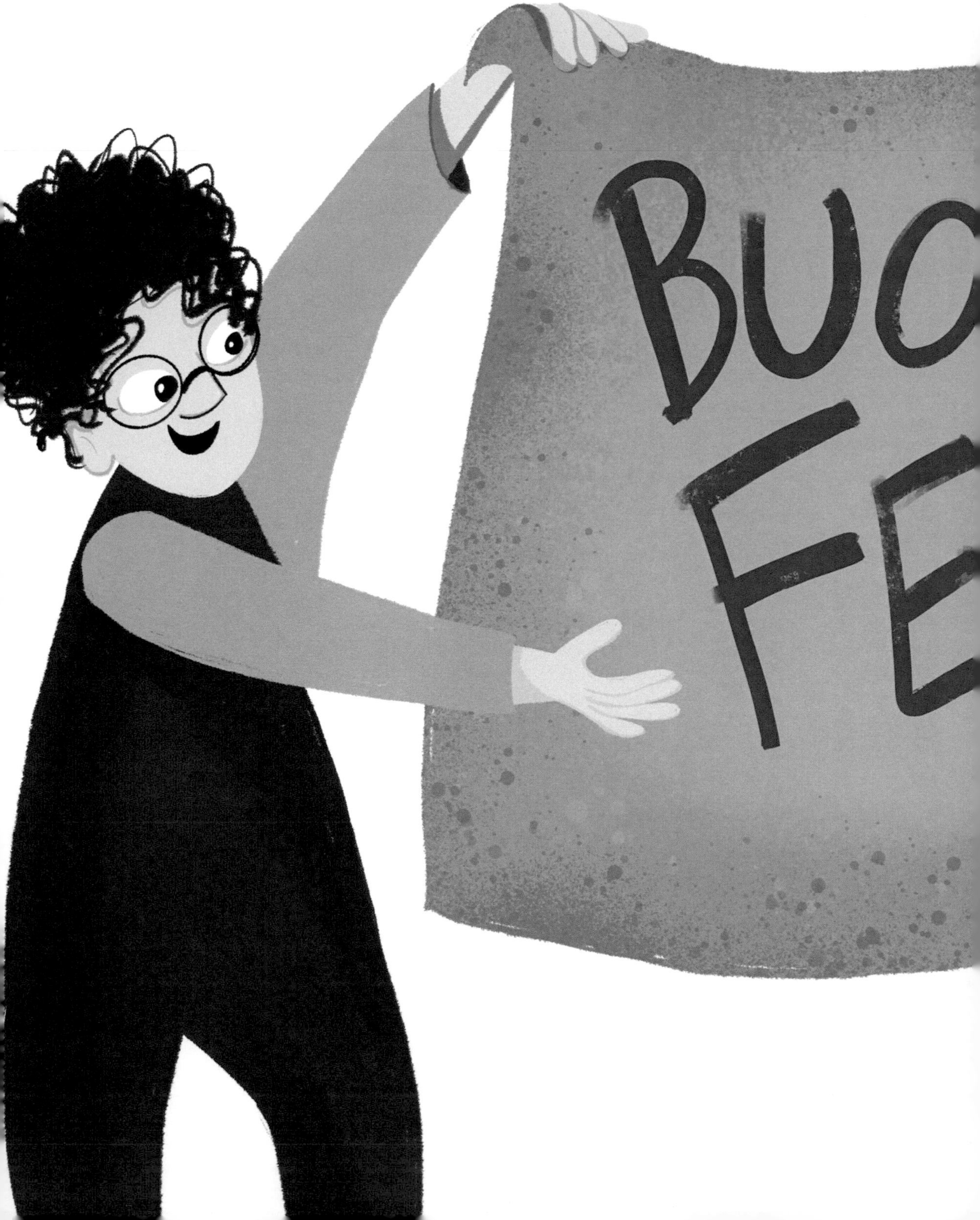
BUO
FE

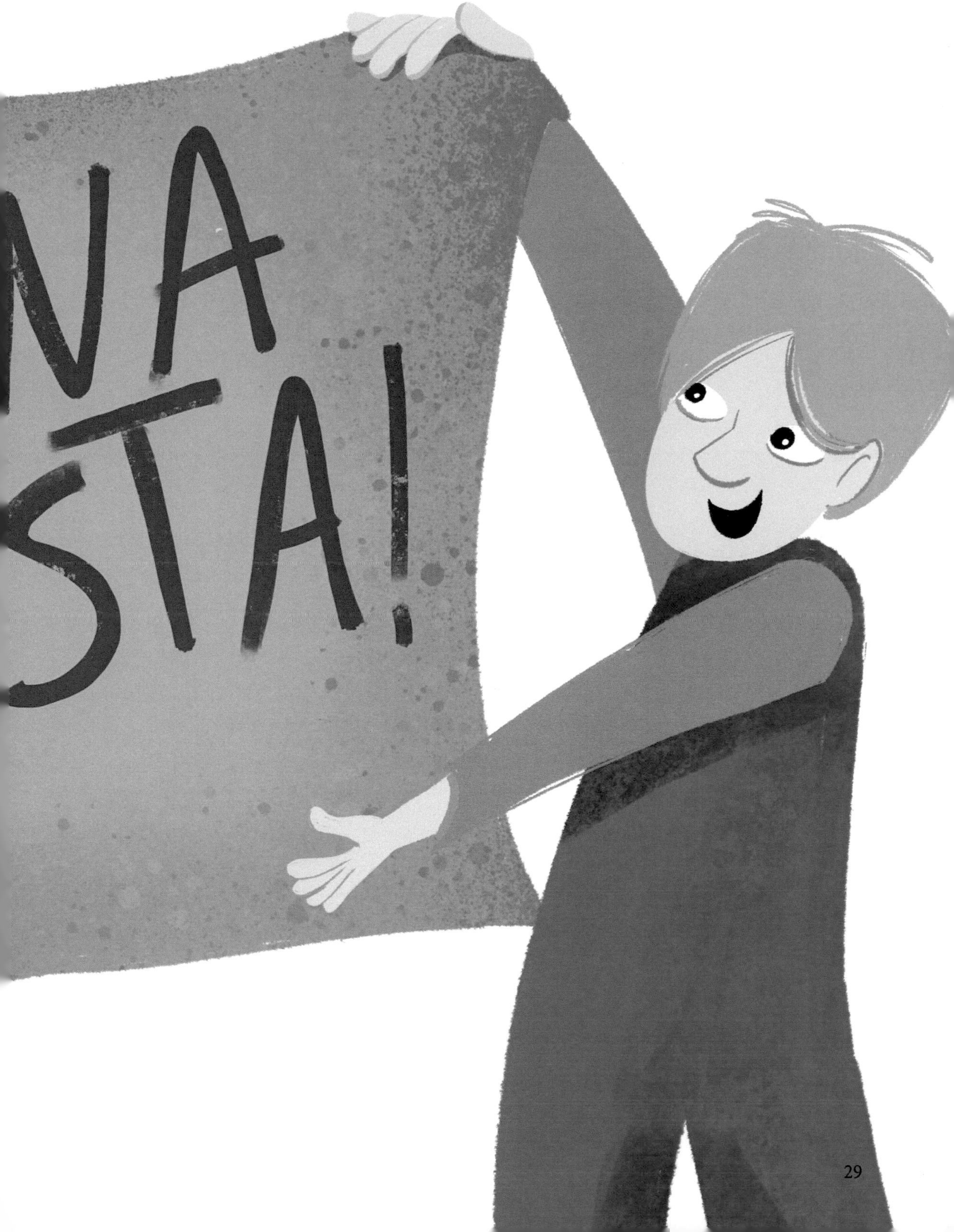
NA
STA!

Feast of the 7 Fishes

Italians celebrate the "Feast of the 7 Fishes" traditionally on Christmas Eve.

The ancient tradition of eating fish on Christmas Eve goes all the way back to the Roman Catholic custom of not eating meat on the eve of certain holidays, including Christmas. The beginning of the Feast of the Seven Fishes started in southern Italy. This area, which is surrounded by a beautiful coastline, is known for its seafood for generations. Many people fished there because they could not afford a lot of other food. Italian immigrants brought the tradition to America, and it is still celebrated today.

Some of the fish that is prepared includes fried calamari, anchovies, sardines, whiting, lobster, and shrimp. Sometimes even eel is eaten! Another is baccalà (cod). But the most important ingredient, of course for any Italian meal is being surrounded by family and friends.

Baccala (cod)

You will need Dried, salt cod pieces (soaking it increases the size)

Coldwater (enough to cover the dried fish pieces)

A large container

2- 14 ounce cans dice tomatoes

1 med. Chopped onion

1 Tbsp. Olive Oil

2 cloves garlic, minced

- Rinse the fish and then place in cold water. Allow soaking for 24 hours, changing the water every 6 hours. The goal is to soak the fish until it is not too salty and the flesh is soft.

- Preheat the oven to 350

- Lay the cooked pieces of fish in a 13 x 9 baking dish (a second one may be needed)

- Sautee the onion in the olive oil until it is translucent.

- Add 2 -14 ounce Diced Tomatoes.

- Mince 2 cloves of garlic into the pot.

- Bring to a gentle boil and then simmer for 15 minutes.

- Pour the sauce over the pieces of fish and cover with foil to cook for 30 minutes.

- MANGIA!!!!

Calamari

3 pounds cleaned, frozen squid (calamari)

Sauce: ½ tsp. salt
2 tbsp. Olive Oil   ¼ tsp. black pepper
1 large onion, chopped finely   ½ tsp. Italian seasoning
2 cloves garlic, minced   ½ tsp. basil
1 stalk celery   2-24 ounce cans tomato sauce

- Prepare the sauce so it can be cooking while you process the squid.

- Sauté the onion, garlic, celery in olive oil over low heat until soft. Add the seasonings and cook a few minutes until fragrant. Add the sauce. Bring it to a boil and then turn down to simmer while you prepare the squid. (30 minutes.)

- You will have to defrost the squid for 2 to 3 days in the refrigerator. Then you will rinse all the squid caps under cold water using a colander. (Discard the tentacles.) Cut the caps in two, forming triangles. Gently scrape the inside of each piece with a knife. Put in a separate colander and rinse again.

- Bring the sauce back to a gentle boil. Lay the squid on top of the boiling sauce, piece by piece until all pieces are in. Turn back to simmer, and allow cooking, slowly for 2 hours. You can then transfer to a crockpot to keep warm while you cook your next dish for Christmas Eve.